Hazel Vs PKD

This book was created to raise awareness for children living with an invisible illness such as Kidney disease. This book was NOT written by a medical professional.

Information on Kidney Disease, including PKD, can be found on the NHS website (U.K).

To
Hazel and Jago...

May you forever keep your fire and strength. May you continue to grow into strong, kind, loving humans. My pride in you both is endless. Loving you always,
Mummy.

For every little superhero
living with a disability or
illness.

RED COW

My name is Hazel and I have a superpower!

That's right,
I am...

1

SUPER BRAVE!

2

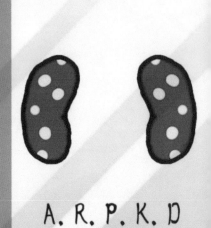

I was born with a
condition called A.R.P.K.D.

3

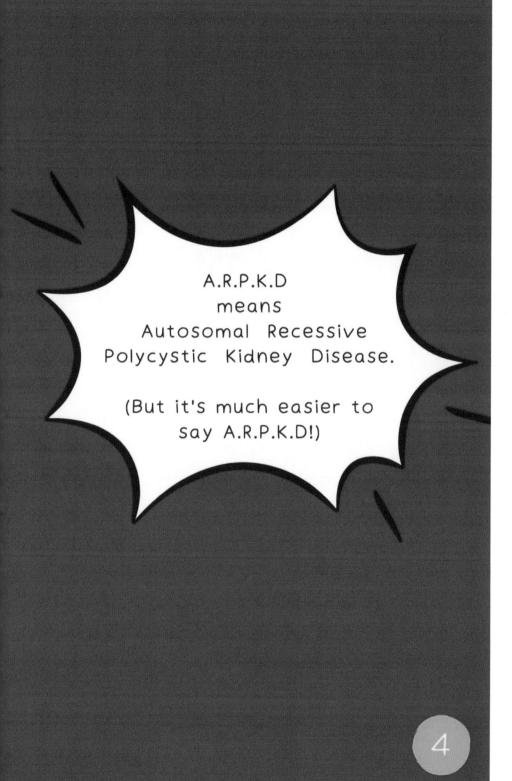

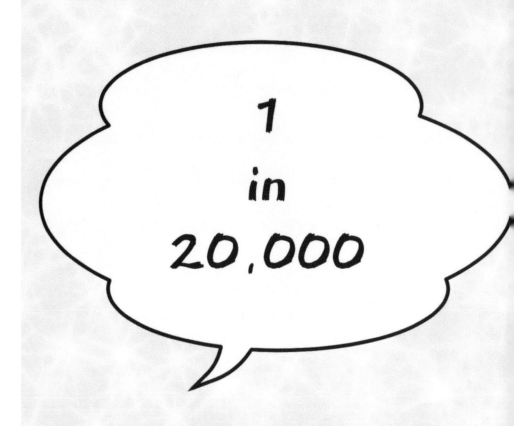

Only one in twenty-thousand children are born with A.R.P.K.D, but I am one of the millions of children around the world with an illness or disability!

Some people have illnesses and disabilities that we can't see, so it's important to always be kind and understanding!

Samiya has diabetes, and Niles has heart disease.

6

PKD is a type of
KIDNEY DISEASE.
This means my kidneys are
poorly and don't work the way
that they should.

Kidneys are found inside our
tummies and have a really
important job.

They help to clear out any
baddies in our bodies and they
make sure the good stuff goes
into our blood to help our
bodies to stay healthy.

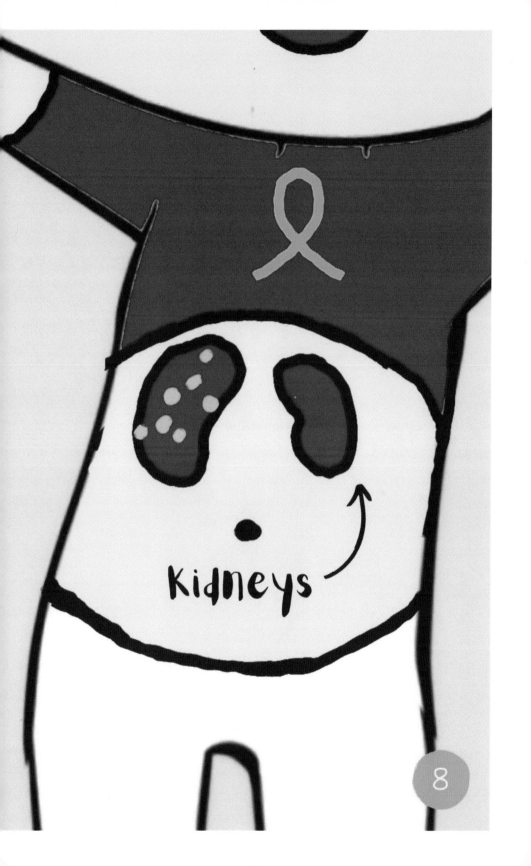

kidneys

8

Those red things are KIDNEYs!
(The ones with the spots are mine).

Those spots are called CYSTS, they
are full of liquid.

The cysts make my kidneys bigger,
which means my tummy is lovely and
round!

The other kidney is one without PKD,
like my brother's.

I spend a lot of time in the HOSPITAL. Sometimes I have sleepovers and get to sleep in the special hospital beds!

I'm not scared of the hospital because I Know that I go there to get better!

The DOCTORS and NURSES do a
lot of tests so that they can see
how well my Kidneys are worKing.

One day my Kidneys will get too
tired and I will need new ones.

11

Whilst I'm waiting for my check-up, the nurses put a MAGIC CREAM on my arm.

The cream has to stay on for a while to work!

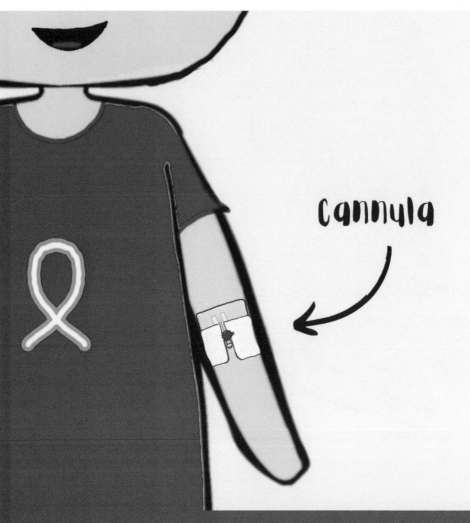

cannula

Once the cream has been on for a while, the doctors put a CANNULA in my arm.

The cannula lets the doctors give me medicine or take blood for my check-up!

The magic cream makes my arm nice and numb. I can't feel a thing so it doesn't hurt, even if it's a bit scary!

13

95 cm

The nurse checks my HEIGHT
(this means how tall I am).
I am little for my age but I don't
mind because I know everyone is
different!

We all come in different shapes
and sizes!

14

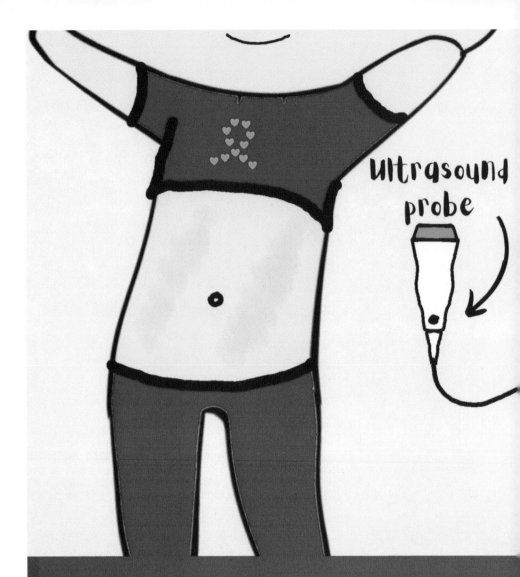

Ultrasound probe

The doctors use an ULTRASOUND MACHINE to look inside my tummy!

They use COLD JELLY to help the wand move smoothly around my tummy. It tickles but I try to keep as still as a statue!

Sometimes I don't feel so super brave and that's OK. Being poorly is really hard and our bodies need time to rest!

And if I rest...

17

DO NOT TOUCH MEDICINE WITHOUT AN ADULT!

...take the MEDICINE the doctor gave me...

water

And stay HYDRATED!
(Because drinking water is
SUPER important for our
bodies)...

I will be back to playing...

20

And feeling
SUPER BRAVE
in no time.

Information for adults

"Autosomal recessive polycystic kidney disease (ARPKD) is a rare inherited childhood condition where the development of the kidneys and liver is abnormal. Over time, either one of these organs may fail. The condition often causes serious problems soon after birth, although less severe cases may not become obvious until a child is older.
ARPKD can cause a wide range of problems, including:

- underdeveloped lungs, which can cause severe breathing difficulties soon after birth
- high blood pressure (hypertension)
- excessive peeing and thirst
- problems with blood flow through the liver, which can lead to serious internal bleeding
- a progressive loss of kidney function, known as chronic kidney disease (CKD)

When these problems develop and how severe they are can vary considerably, even between family members with the condition.

Even though ARPKD is rare, it's one of the most common kidney problems to affect young children. It's estimated around 1 in 20,000 babies is born with the condition. Both boys and girls are affected equally."

-SOURCE: NHS ENGLAND

Charities to support

Below is a list of UK Charities dedicated to funding research into Kidney Disease.

- PKD Charity UK
- Kidney Research UK
- Kidney Care UK
- UK Kidney Association

Printed in Great Britain
by Amazon